Pent Up!

RICH BOTTLES JR.

Therefore, let us stop passing judgment on one another.
Instead, make up your mind not to put any stumbling block
or obstacle in the way of a brother or sister.
--- Romans 14:13

Burning Bulb
PUBLISHING

Pent Up!
By **Rich Bottles Jr.**

Burning Bulb Publishing
P.O. Box 4721
Bridgeport, WV 26330-4721
United States of America
www.BurningBulbPublishing.com

Cover designed by Gary Lee Vincent and Rich Bottles Jr. with photos from Cecilia Ochotorena and Donald Tong from Pexels.

First Edition.

Paperback Edition ISBN: 978-1-948278-40-9

Printed in the United States of America

SEVENFOLD

The Power of Jesus,
The Power of Jesus,
The Power of Jesus,
The Power of Jesus,
The Power of Jesus,
The Power of Jesus,
The Power of Jesus,
The Spirit of the Lord shall rest upon me
The Spirit of wisdom and understanding
The Spirit of counsel
The Spirit of might
The Spirit of knowledge,
And the fear of the Lord!
These are the spirits,
The spirits of God,
These are the spirits,
Held by our Lord!
The Power of Jesus,
The Power of Jesus,
The Power of Jesus,
The Power of Jesus,
The Power of Jesus,
The Power of Jesus,
The Power of Jesus,
Sevenfold!!!!!!!

PROLOGUE

Yeah, that was me, Ross Blakely, sitting alone at the Rooster Inn Bar in South Tucson, Arizona. I was staring at my drink because I couldn't stand looking around at all those people having a good time. I had a lot on my mind, you see. A hell of a lot.

I'd just found out a couple days ago from my older sister that my fifteen-year-old niece had been missing for two months. The police didn't have a clue where the kid was and probably didn't give a damn.

So, my holy-roller sister finally got around to calling me after she realized that her prayers and her calls to the cops weren't going to bring her brat back. She knew the dark life I led and the shady characters I associated with. She understood that I was probably the only chance she had for finding her precious Jenny.

You see, I was a mob enforcer. If some welcher didn't want to pay back his loan shark or some stoolie squealed on his partners, then I'd get a call and I would fix the situation... Now you know why I was sitting alone at the bar on that life-changing day.

CHAPTER 1

But what you don't know is how I ended up in a six-by-six foot cubical inside the Assemblies of Christ Ministries office in Grantsville, Maryland. Believe me, the numerical significance of being six feet tall, and working in a six by six space, has not escaped me. But my whole life has been about escaping the dark side.

This particular morning, I was holding a framed family portrait that I kept beside my monitor on my cluttered desk. The picture featured my tattooed mug, alongside the smiling faces of my sister Samantha and my niece Jennifer. Just by the mere existence of this portrait, you should be able to surmise that I successfully rescued Jenny from the drug dealers that she had holed up with in Tucson.

Of course, I didn't rescue her alone. There was some, let's say, Divine Intervention involved that saved both my niece and me. When these drug dealers left me to die out in the cold Arizona desert, I looked up to the clear starry skies of Heaven and begged God to save me from an almost certain fate.

Considering that was probably the first time I mentioned God's name, without it being spoken in vain, my desperate plea was heard that night. A mysterious passerby found my beaten and bound body, and delivered me to my sister's church. I soon accepted Jesus Christ into my heart - and the rest (e.g., my sordid past) is history.

Although my niece agreed to return home only if I promised to always stay there with her and her mother, even Jenny realized my promise wouldn't be possible considering the eventual publicity surrounding her rescue. A book and a movie, entitled Strange Friends, by a fellow named Gary Lee Vincent, soon emerged detailing my family's ordeal, and I couldn't seem to escape the unwelcome notoriety.

I then got the calling/opportunity to work for the Lord here at the Assemblies of Christ Ministries in Maryland. But I sure miss my sister and niece!

"Hey, Ross, I brought you some coffee," announced the office receptionist, as she peeked around the entryway of my cubicle.

She brought in a steaming paper cup of black coffee and placed it on the only empty space on my desk. Now I no longer had a place to set the picture frame in my hand.

"You didn't have to do that, Julia," I said. "I'm perfectly capable of getting my own coffee from the break room."

"Well, I noticed you seemed preoccupied with something when you came in this morning and failed to greet me."

"Oh, did I forget to tell you good morning?"

Actually, Julia seemed busy when I entered the office and I thought she didn't see me come in...

"Yep, you walked right past me without saying a word."

"I'm sorry about that Julia," I apologized. "I guess something was on my mind."

"You're not dating anyone are you?" she inquired with a frown.

"No, Julia," I assured her. "I still haven't forgotten your gracious invitation to show me around Garrett County."

"I wasn't referring to that," she referred. "By the way, if you had cordially greeted me this morning, I would've told you about the gentleman who came by the office earlier and asked to speak with you."

"There's someone here who wants to speak to me?"

"Uh-huh, there sure is."

"Well, please send him in, Julia," I pleaded. "Let's not keep the man waiting any longer."

"He's not in the office," she explained. "He said he would prefer to wait out by the lighthouse."

Although the Assemblies of Christ Ministries has a large lighthouse that extends out toward Route 68, there are no bodies of water near Grantsville. The functioning lighthouse simply serves as a metaphor to attract lost souls, sort of like that steel-framed unfinished Ark just up the road.

When I stepped out onto the lighthouse walkway, which juts out like a partial bridge toward the interstate, I noticed a lone man in tattered work clothes with his back toward me. I glanced backward at the church parking lot, expecting to see a horse and Amish buggy.

As I walked closer to the man, he turned around and got startled by my appearance and proximity. The frightened middle-aged man put up his hands like he was trying to fend off a demon.

"Hey there, fella, I don't want no trouble," he called to me.

"Nor do I, my friend," I greeted, trying my best to project a welcoming smile. "My name is Ross Blakely. I believe you came here to see me?"

He cautiously extended his hand to shake.

"Sorry, Mister Blakely, I guess I imagined you as looking differ'nt. My name is William Crisp and I am from the unincorporated village of Metz, West Virginia."

Keeping eye contact, I firmly shook his rough, calloused hand and commented, "West by God Virginia, eh? So, what brings you to Maryland?"

"I'd like to speak with you about some goings on at my church," he explained.

"Well, I'd be happy to discuss your church, but I'd like to suggest we go inside and sit down. I can get us a private conference room."

"That would suit me just fine, Mister Blakely."

As I turned around to lead the way back to the office, I assured him, "Okay then, follow me... Also, you can call me Ross."

I rolled my eyes when I heard him respond from behind: "An' you can call me, Mister Crisp."

Once *Mister* Crisp was seated in a small conference room, I offered, "Would you like some coffee, Mister Crisp?"

"No sir," he declined. "I try to avoid caffeine drinks. But thank you anyways."

"I apologize, sir," I apologized. "Sometimes I forget that different churches have different restrictions on food and drink."

"Nah, it ain't that," he explained. "I jus' personally avoid caffeine and other stimulants."

I smiled and added, "Well, not all stimulants are bad, Mister Crisp. Do you mind if I fetch my coffee?"

"Suit yerself."

When I returned from my cube with the coffee, I noticed Mister Crisp praying silently with his head down and hands crossed. I respectfully closed the conference room door.

I pulled out the chair opposite Mister Crisp and quietly sat down. He opened his eyes and studied me for a bit, then concluded, "Yes, siree, you sure got some innerestin' tattoos, 'specially all over yer face."

"Well..." I began.

"An' what's that say 'cross yer knuckles?"

I noticed he could see my knuckles by the way I held my coffee cup. I subconsciously loosened my grip on the cup... By the way, if you were to read my knuckles from left to right, you would notice the unfortunate phrase of EVIL F*CK.

"As I was going to say, I got these tattoos long before I became Born Again."

"Well, kint you git them removed?" he exclaimed.

"I probably could," I admitted. "But it would be expensive - not to mention painful, especially across my face. Plus, it would probably leave scars."

He promptly ignored my explanation.

"And I thought thirteen was an unlucky number," he observed. "But you gotta a big thirteen right across yer cheek!"

"I'm also keeping the tattoos because sometimes I need reminded of the sinful life I used to lead, before asking Jesus Christ into my life," I tried again.

"Okay," he acquiesced. "Well, I'm glad yer now a Christian."

"So am I," I sighed. "But enough about me. Let's talk about your church, Mister Crisp."

"You kin call me Bill," he said with a smile.

I smiled back at Bill and said, "How can the Assemblies of Christ help you, Bill?"

"Well, I'd like to know if you've been receivin' the letters I sent you," he inquired.

"Letters?" I asked. "You sent me letters?"

"Well, I dint sign them, of course," he answered, "but I did send them directly to you."

"Yeah, Bill," I suddenly remembered. "I've been receiving a number of anonymous letters lately from West Virginia."

"Welp, those would be from me," he admitted. "What d'ya think of 'em?"

"Well, if I can recall," I recalled. "The letters contain some troubling accusations about a Pentecostal preacher down your way."

"Yep, it's troublin' all right," he added with a nod.

"Troubling or not," I explained, "you have to understand that neither I nor the Assemblies of Christ are going to investigate accusations made anonymously. That would not be fair to the accused."

"That's why I'm here," he proclaimed. "No more animity!"

Knowing the true meaning of the word he mispronounced, I lowered my head and mumbled, "Ah yes, the state of one's soul."

"Scuse me?"

I looked back up to Bill's confused face and reminded him, "Nothing, Bill... You came all this way to talk to me about your church and the pastor, so let's hear it."

"All right," he answered. "Preacher Ripley done whipped my daughter with a belt."

I was about to sip some coffee when the shock caused me to interject, "The pastor beat your daughter?!"

Bill's voice began to break as he reiterated, "Yes, sir, he did... An' she's only twelve years old."

"It doesn't matter how old she is," I emphatically stated. "No man of the cloth should be physically disciplining someone else's child."

"Well, that's the thing, Ross," he explained. "I think my wife gave the preacher permission."

I shook my head in disbelief. "Without consulting you?"

"Yes," he answered, "and I might not ever have learned of it, except I asked my daughter why she was actin' so sullen. She tole me that she got the Devil whipped outta her 'cause she was misbehavin' at church."

"You're sure she wasn't making it up?" I cautioned. "I mean, kids her age..."

"She showed me the welts."

I sat dumbfounded for a moment, then responded, "Okay, then, did you confront your wife about it?"

"Yes, sir, I did," he admitted. "But she acted like it was no big deal and said I should-ah recognized that my daughter was possessed by a demon."

"No big deal, eh?" I responded. "Does your wife realize that child services have taken away children for less?"

"In our county, nobody involves the state in anything... and I sorta agree."

"Well, I wasn't suggesting calling in the state to investigate," I explained.

"'Cause that's what you're here for, right?"

I paused and answered, "Yes, Bill, the Assemblies of Christ does perform investigations, if you can call it that."

"I do call it that," he confirmed.

"Okay, Bill, but we're not a regulatory agency. For instance, we can't just remove a pastor from a church."

"Then what good are ya?" he snarled.

"Well, Bill, we can *investigate* certain accusations, as you would call it," I admitted. "And if we find problems, we can make recommendations to the church elders or trustees... Actually, strong recommendations..."

Bill interrupted, "So you'll come down and check on the Pentecostal Church of Metz?"

I reluctantly agreed, "Sure Bill, I'll drop by for a service or two, and I'll speak with the pastor and some other church members."

Bill reached over and grabbed the inked hands he had seemed so enamored with earlier.

"Thank you," he cried. "Thank you, so much!"

"You're welcome, Bill," I answered, now more assured of my decision to visit Metz.

"Just don't tell anyone I sent you," he added.

I assured him, "Bill, I will hold our meeting in complete confidence."

"I told my wife I was going out of town on important business," he confessed.

I raised a brow and asked, "So, you lied to your wife?"

"No, sir," he declared. "This *is* important business."

Bill then stood up and took his leave from the conference room, leaving me and my coffee to occupy the space. I grabbed the cup and took a sip, causing me to grimace and glance down at the stale black liquid.

"It's cold as hell, of course."

CHAPTER 2

Not meaning to cop out on this first-person narrative, but the following is sworn testimony from a witness of what occurred at the Metz Pentecostal Church prior to my belated arrival:

Although the pews were full, the Metz Pentecostal Church was quiet, with maybe a baby making a fuss here and there. There was a wooden podium/pulpit in the front center of a small stage.

A man holding an acoustic guitar, named Brother Andrew, was seated toward the back of the stage, along with two women, sisters Dee and Winnie Williams, who were sitting next to the guitarist.

Beside the pulpit was an empty aquarium, with a mysterious purple glass bottle setting on the lid.

In attendance were many church regulars, including the Crisp family, the Jeffreys family, and diner regular Robert Brown.

Pastor Harry Ripley entered the sanctuary from the back of the church and slowly made his way toward the pulpit. Ripley made a point of resting his hand on the shoulders of a few parishioners as he passed, asking them questions loud enough for everyone to hear.

Ripley: "Brother Thomas, how can one enter the Kingdom of God?"

Brother Thomas: "Truly I tell you; you must be Born Again!"

The pastor walked farther up the aisle and placed his hand on the shoulder of Sister Mercy.

Ripley: "Sister Mercy, how can one see the angels of Heaven?"

Sister Mercy: "Truly I tell you; you must be Born Again!"

The pastor continued up the aisle, placing his hand on Brother Arthur.

Ripley: "How would one escape death and have everlasting life?"

Brother Arthur: "Truly I tell you; you must be Born Again!"

The pastor approached Brother James in the front pew and rested a palm on the man's shoulder.

Ripley: "Brother James, how is one forgiven of their sins?"

Brother James: "Truly I tell you; you must be Born Again!"

Pastor Ripley then reached the pulpit, stepping behind the wooden podium, and boldly proclaiming: "Truly I Tell You, Jesus Christ is Lord!"

A few scattered "Amens" were heard from the pews as Ripley turned his head backward toward the sisters on stage. "Isn't that right, sisters?!"

The sisters stood and began slowly chanting:
"Truly I Tell You,
Truly I Tell You,
Truly I Tell You,
Jesus Christ is Lord!"

Still turned toward the sisters, Ripley asked again, "What was that sisters? I can hardly hear you!"

The sisters raised their voices and began clapping in rhythm with the song:

"Truly I Tell You,
Truly I Tell You,
Truly I Tell You,
Jesus Christ is Lord!"

Addressing the guitarist, who was seated on a stool beside the sisters, Ripley asked, "What about you, Brother Andrew, on the guitar?! Do you have anything to add?!"

Brother Andrew suddenly leapt from the stool, landing firmly on the stage while strumming power chords from his beaten-up acoustic six-string. As the tempo dramatically increased, the pastor, the Williams sisters and the whole congregation enthusiastically burst into song and dance. Spinning, jumping, stomping, with arms waving in the air, everyone participated in a rousing rendition of the church's original hymn called, "Truly I Tell You":

You can't see the Kingdom
The Kingdom of God
You can't see that Kingdom,
Unless you're Born Again!
You can't see no Angels
Ascend or Descend
You can't see no Heaven,
Unless you're Born Again!
Truly I Tell You
Truly I Tell You
Truly I Tell You
Jesus Christ is Lord!
Like a kernel of wheat

That falls to the ground
You'll stay only a seed,
Unless you're Born Again!
While the world rejoices
You will weep and mourn
'Cause death is coming,
Unless you're Born Again!
Truly I Tell You
Truly I Tell You
Truly I Tell You
Jesus Christ is Lord!
I know I'm a sinner
A slave to my sins
But I can't repent,
Unless I'm Born Again!
So, bring me the water
Bring me the Spirit
I can't be forgiven,
Unless I'm Born Again!
Truly I Tell You
Truly I Tell You
Truly I Tell You
Jesus Christ is Lord!

As the chorus repeated over and over, the congregation seemed to erupt into utter chaos. No one remained seated or still. In fact, some folks fell to the floor, writhing and twisting their bodies to the maddening rhythm. There was also ear-shattering shrieking, and red-faced screaming in tongues, as parishioners seemed to lose all control over their convulsing bodies. One man was seen drinking from the mysterious bottle, while a woman performed numerous cartwheels/backflips up the center aisle.

Then I walked in, and everything ground to a dramatic halt.

Everyone turned their heads toward me and stared. Yes, they all stared silently at me as though I was some kind of alien dropping in from outer space... Maybe a kin to the Point Pleasant Mothman or the Flatwoods Monster?

I didn't know how to respond or react to the *horror picture show* unfolding before me, so I blurted out the only thing I could think of: "Say, do one of you guys know how to Madison?"

No one found my comment funny and they all continued to blankly stare at me. Pastor Ripley eventually saved my ass. He spread his arms wide at the pulpit and began laughing heartily. One or two others followed his lead and began chuckling, then everyone else seemed to join in.

"Welcome to our humble church, sir!" Ripley welcomed me. "Please come in and find a seat! We're about to begin tonight's sermon!"

I, of course, took the first seat that I saw empty in the back pew.

"Um, thank you," I humbly announced. "Please don't let me interrupt."

Once the congregation members found their seats, Ripley wiped his brow with a handkerchief and began his sermon:

"One of the true pioneers of the Independent Pentecostal movement was a man named Stanley

Frodsham. Mistrust and misjudgment seemed to follow Brother Frodsham wherever he ministered, whether it be Britain, Canada or America. But he always kept the faith and was recognized as a prophet in 1965 when he addressed the Elim Bible Institute in Lima, New York, at the age of eighty-three. Who here tonight is prepared to hear what Brother Frodsham had to say?"

As if on cue, members of the congregation belted out pleas of "Tell us!", "We're prepared!" and "What is the prophecy?!"

Ripley complied:

"Let me ask you somethin'! When Jesus Christ returns, who do you think he's gonna judge first? The deviants in the penitentiary? Hell no!"

"Hell no!" the congregation echoed.

"The heathens teachin' our kids?"

"Hell no!" the congregation answered.

"The lyin' thievin' politicians?"

"Hell no!"

"The prostitutes walkin' the streets?"

"Hell no!"

"The drug dealers pushing their damn meth?"

"Hell no!"

"The murderin' abortionists?"

"Hell no!"

You get the drift, right?

Ripley then confirmed, "Hell no, is right! When Jesus Christ returns, he is first gonna clean up His own house!"

"Amen!" was the communal response.

Now the pastor was really working up a head of spiritual steam:

"Before Jesus visits the nations in judgment, He will begin at His house! Then when His wrath does come upon the cities of the world, His people shall be separate! Jesus desires His people to be without spot or wrinkle, and such shall be preserved when His wrath rains down upon all iniquity and unrighteousness!

"As you seek Jesus, He will open up truths to you that you have not seen before; and these very truths will be that which will enable you to stand in the last days! As you are persecuted, reviled, and rejected by your brethren, you will turn unto Jesus with all your heart and seek Him for that spiritual life you need! When tribulation comes, you will have that which will enable you to stand on solid ground while others shall be tossed about like a tugboat within a turbulent torrent! For the end times shall be very terrible, the likes of which has never been seen before! Yes, you may listen to the messengers, but do not hold these men in admiration! Jesus calls many into His ministry, but remember that many of these men shall also fall! They shall be like bright lights, and the people shall delight in them, but they shall be taken over by deceiving spirits and shall lead many of Jesus's people astray!"

I remember checking my wristwatch at some point, shocked that the pastor could sustain such a fiery and furious message for what seemed like hours. But he did.

"Though Satan may come as an angel of light, hearken not to him for he is not righteous! Look unto Jesus and He will allow you to perceive with the eyes of the Holy Spirit the things that lurk in darkness and that are not visible to the human eye! Let Jesus lead you in this way that you may perceive the powers of darkness and battle against them! For it is not a battle against flesh and blood! It is a battle against the powers of darkness and for the liberation of Jesus's people!"

Although the pastor's pocket handkerchief was already drenched in perspiration, he still attempted to dry off his sweaty brow with the cloth. The scattered proclamations of "Amen!" once again echoed throughout the sanctuary.

Ripley now stood almost still at the pulpit, trying hard to catch his breath. His pounding chest and heavy breathing had me concerned that he may need medical assistance. But he regained his composure after a minute or so.

Much more calmly and softly, he then bespoke, "Of course, Jesus also said blessed are the children, and I think it would be fitting for one of our children to close today's service by singing a song that she composed, based on an old children's standard... Please come up to the altar, Miss Amber."

The Crisp girl shyly left her family's pew and approached the pulpit. Ripley came out from behind the wooden podium, gently turned her to face the congregation, and lightly placed his palms atop her small shoulders. She was holding a sheet of paper in her somewhat trembling hands.

From behind her, Ripley announced, "Amber, it's my understanding that you wrote these new lyrics because you thought the song's original words were mean-spirited."

Amber turned her head and looked up at the pastor, answering, "Yes, sir. My song is called, Satan Don't Bother Me!"

Ripley now turned toward Brother Andrew and asked, "I assume you know the song, Shoo Fly Don't Bother Me?"

"Yes, sir!" Brother Andrew answered. "We done practiced it!"

Ripley stepped back from the girl and concluded, "All right then, let's hear it!"

Amber sang resoundingly, as though she had always been destined to sing this song, while the strumming of the guitar and the clapping of the congregation complemented her perfectly:

I think I hear the angels sing
I think I hear the angels sing
I think I hear the angels sing
The angels now are on the wing.
I feel, I feel, I feel
That's what my mother said
The angels pouring blessings down
Upon this sinner's head.
Strychnine don't bother me
Strychnine don't bother me
Strychnine don't bother me
For God protects my young body.
I feel, I feel, I feel,
I feel like a blessed child

I feel, I feel, I feel,
I feel like a blessed child
I feel, I feel, I feel,
I feel like a blessed child
I feel, I feel, I feel,
I feel like a blessed child.
If I believe in Jesus Christ
If I believe in Jesus Christ
If I believe in Jesus Christ
The angels now are on the rise.
I feel, I feel, I feel
That's what my mother said.
The angels pouring blessings down
Upon this sinner's head.
Venom don't bother me
Venom don't bother me
Venom don't bother me
For God protects my young body.
I feel, I feel, I feel,
I feel like a blessed child
I feel, I feel, I feel,
I feel like a blessed child
I feel, I feel, I feel,
I feel like a blessed child
I feel, I feel, I feel,
I feel like a blessed child.

The congregation, of course, gave Amber a standing ovation, including myself, although I may have been the last person to stand. In fact, many members of the church looked around to make sure I was standing and ovating.

"That was awesome, Miss Amber!" declared Ripley. "Feel free to sing for us any time!"

Pastor Ripley eventually made his way out of the church the same way he had entered, walking down the center aisle, like Moses crossing the Red Sea. Once he took his place just outside the doors of the church, the congregation began leaving. Ripley made small talk as the people exited, mostly accepting thanks and appreciation for the sermon, while responding "Bless you", "You're welcome," "See you next time," etc.

I was the last to leave the church and the last to shake the pastor's hand.

"That was quite a stirring sermon, I must admit," I admitted.

"You missed the best part when we praised God at the beginning," Ripley pointed out.

"Well, the location of your church proved to be more off-the-beaten-path than I expected."

"Regardless," he concluded with a smile, "I'm glad you found us. It's always good to see new faces!"

"Even ones that are covered in tattoos?" I asked.

"Especially the ones that are covered in tattoos!" he exclaimed.

"Well," I introduced, "in case you haven't figured it out, I'm Ross Blakely, who called you from the Assemblies of Christ Ministries."

"I figgered as much," he admitted. "I'd invite you in to talk tonight, but it's getting late and sometimes it takes me a while to wind down after a sermon."

"Completely understood!" I replied. "And I look forward to speaking with you tomorrow. In fact, I plan on grabbing a late dinner tonight and checking into the motel off the interstate. You have a good evening."

"You too, brother… You too."

CHAPTER 3

I drove directly to a local eatery called Phyllis's Diner, but found the small parking lot to be full of vehicles, which I thought was odd considering the late hour, but then I realized there was probably not much else to do in Metz during the evening.

I parked in an adjacent lot, but had to walk through a dark alleyway to reach the restaurant. As I transversed the alley, I did not allow the aroma of rotting dumpster debris to deter my burgeoning appetite.

When I entered the diner, I took a seat at the counter once I noticed that all the booths were packed with loud-talking patrons (yes, many talked while they chewed). Actually, I was quite pleased that no one stopped talking when they saw me enter.

A scowling dingy-aproned waitress soon approached me from behind the counter, notepad and pencil ready in hand.

"You want this order to go?"

"Excuse me? What?"

"I'm guessin' you want this order to go," she guessed.

"Well, you guessed wrong," I answered, slightly perturbed. "May I please have a menu?"

She grabbed a soiled menu from beneath the counter and dropped it in front of me.

"Sure thing, hun," she responded. "I suppose you want something to drink?"

"A coffee would be fine," I ordered. "Thank you."

"Sure thing, hun."

As soon as the waitress left the counter to fetch me some coffee, I heard a woman bellowing from the booth behind me.

"Hey, fella! Ain't you that outsider who came to our church tonight?!"

I turned around on the convenient rotating stool and smiled at the inquisitive individual and her guests. "Indeed, I was," I answered. "And I am so glad that your church welcomes outsiders like me."

The woman's face reddened with embarrassment and she responded, "Oh... Well, welcome, I guess."

As I spun my stool back around, I came face-to-face with the waitress as she was placing the coffee cup/saucer on the counter.

"You decided yet?" she inquired.

I handed the menu back and acquiesced, "Actually, if you got a hamburger and fries, that would be fine."

"Sure thing, hun."

I barely got down a mouthful of lukewarm coffee when another local approached me, taking a seat on the stool beside me. He looked like one of those insurance salesmen who never developed a personality.

Offering me his clammy hand, he forced a half smile, and greeted, "Hello, my name is Robert Brown. I was at the service tonight too."

And, no, I didn't lie when I responded, "I seem to recognize you."

I shook his hand and revealed, "My name is Ross Blakely."

"Nice to meet you," he probably lied.

"That was quite a rousing sermon minister Ripley gave tonight."

"You missed the best part when we praised God at the beginning," Brown pointed out.

"Ah, yeah, the pastor mentioned that to me."

Brown leaned closer into my space and whispered, "By the way, please excuse the good Sister behind you. I hope you weren't offended by her outsider comment."

"That?" I feigned. "No, of course not."

"Because it's not that we don't like outsiders around here," he explained. "It's that we don't never get any outsiders around here."

I took another drink of coffee (because you gotta drink it when you have a chance, right?) and reassured him, "I completely understand."

He waited until I placed the cup back onto the saucer, then bluntly inquired, "So why are you here exactly?"

I glanced at him. "Why am I here in Metz, you ask?"

"Yeah," he confirmed.

"Well, I represent the Assemblies of Christ Ministries," I said with a smile. "And it's not unusual for AoC members to drop by small churches to better understand what's going on within the community of Christ."

"Is that right?" he challenged without smiling.

"Yes," I expounded. "And if a small church needs help with something, the Assemblies can often provide assistance."

Brown raised an eyebrow, I don't remember which one, and he asked, "What's the Assemblies think about preaching the signs of Mark Sixteen?"

I nonchalantly added, "You mean, verses seventeen and eighteen?"

Brown lit up and answered, "Yeah, you know what I'm talkin' about!"

"Well, Mister Brown," I testified, "since I don't represent law enforcement, I will tell you that I believe churches should be free to praise God in any manner they see fit, as long as it doesn't cause any harm."

"Then you ain't worried about nobody gettin' bit by a snake or gettin' sick from drinkin' poison?" he charged.

"According to Mark Sixteen, God should protect against that. Right, Mister Brown?"

"Damn, right!" he proclaimed.

"And according to the First Amendment of the U.S. Constitution, the government shall make no law respecting an establishment of religion, or prohibiting the free exercise thereof. Right, Mister Brown?"

"Right!" he emphatically agreed.

"So, I guess your church and Pastor Ripley have nothing to worry about," I concluded.

He contemplated a response for a few seconds and then pointed out, "Pastor Ripley is a good man."

"I never said he wasn't."

CHAPTER 4

It was pretty late when I arrived at the Interstate Motel, but thankfully they left the light on for me. It was one of those single-level retro places where all the doors opened onto the parking lot.

I was promptly greeted by a nondescript Desk Clerk when I entered the smallish lobby.

"The sign outside says you have a vacancy," I observed.

"We always have a vacancy," the clerk confirmed.

"Well, that works out for me," I said as I approached the counter.

"Used to be the only night we'd be full was on Prom night," the clerk expounded.

"Did the school stop having prom?" I asked without really caring.

"Nah," answered the clerk. "Preacher Ripley started comin' 'round on Prom night with his bull horn, trying to shame the kids from fornicatin'."

"Oh, but maybe it was for the best."

"Not good for business though," admitted the clerk

"I guess not," I agreed. "But hey, I just need a room for the night."

The Desk Clerk studied me for a moment and then inquired, "Is there a Juggalo convention in town?"

I crooked my head slightly to the side to indicate that I was more annoyed than amused.

"What are you implying?" I insisted. "Are you saying I look like a clown?"

The challenged clerk took an unsteady step back from the counter and answered, "No, sir. We just don't get a lot of out-of-towners here."

"You run a motel next to an interstate, but you're telling me you don't get many people from out of town?"

"Like I said," the clerk said with a nervous smile, "we always have vacancies."

"Yeah, so can you please hook me up with a room?"

"Of course, I can," the clerk agreed. "Let me get you set up right away."

"Thank you kindly."

The Desk Clerk pulled out a piece of paper and carefully explained the contents, going paragraph by paragraph, as though I couldn't read. After using a broken pen as a pointer, the clerk handed the writing implement to me.

"The price of the room is sixty dollars," the clerk instructed. "If you would initial there by the price... and also there, where it says you won't take anythin'."

Initially, I rolled my eyes before I initialed. "Just to set your mind at ease, I don't plan on taking anything."

"It's just a standard form, sir," the clerk pointed out. "Also, I'll need to see a form of ID and a credit card."

I pulled out my wallet, unhooking it from the trusty chain on my belt, and removed the appropriate cards. I then obediently handed the cards across the counter.

The Desk Clerk expressed satisfaction with the cards. "Thank you, Mister Blakely. This'll just take a second... I'm going to put you on the far end of the motel... It's quieter there."

The Desk Clerk two-finger-typed some information into an old dusty computer and then handed my cards back, along with a room key. "You're good to go, Mister Blakely. Have a nice evening."

"Thank you again," I repeated.

I then walked toward the lobby door, but suddenly remembered the clerk's earlier snide remark. So, I turned around and asked, "Oh, by the way, does your soda machine carry Faygo?"

And what did I find when I unlocked the door to my room and flicked on the lights? An unmade bed, of course.

"Oh, great," I grumbled.

I then lugged my suitcase into the bathroom to check for used bars of soap and pubic hair, but fortunately found the bathroom to be fairly clean. I walked back out to the disheveled bed and lifted the phone receiver on the nightstand, dialing zero.

"Front desk, how may I help you?"

"Yes, this is Ross Blakely. The bed hasn't been made up in the room you gave me."

"Would you like me to send someone to make it?"

"Well, yes, I'd like the bed to be made up... Of course, I would. Why would you even ask that?"

"Sorry, sir. I'll send someone right away."

"Thank you, I'm going to be getting a shower, so please tell the maid not to enter the bathroom... Yes, the bathroom looks fine. Again, please tell the maid to stay out of the bathroom. I just need fresh linens on the bed."

Of course, I still locked the bathroom door.

Anyway, when I exited the bathroom wearing only my boxers, I was relieved to see the bed had been made, even though the lights had been turned off in the room. Moving cautiously, with the light of the bathroom to guide me, I managed to find my way to the nightstand and to turn on the lamp.

I looked down at the freshly made bed and commented aloud to myself, "Well, that looks better... But I see the maid didn't leave any mints."

"I got something sweet."

Okay, so there I was standing in my motel room, wearing nothing but boxers, and talking to myself (which we all do on occasion, so don't act like you've never done it), when I heard a female voice tell me "I got something sweet." Of course it startled me!

I turned around to see a woman stroll out of the shadows and approach me.

"Like I said, Mister Blakely, I got something sweet."

"I heard you the first time," I responded with annoyance. "Who are you and how'd you get in here?"

She continued to sashay toward me, answering in her most sultry voice, "My name's Eleanor Crisp, sugar. The maid was kind enough to allow me to wait inside for you. I told her that me an' you had a meetin' set up for tonight."

Now I'm sure you've noticed in your reading thus far that I'm not real big on describing the physical appearance of the people involved in this story, because I try not to pass judgment on people's appearance and neither should you; but I will tell you that this middle-aged woman's curvaceous body rocked the tight-fitting red dress she managed to squeeze into.

"And what if I had come out of the bathroom naked?" I stupidly asked.

"You wouldn't hear me complainin', sugar!"

And I've also been careful not to describe my own physique in this story (out of modesty, of course). For instance, I could've described my earlier shower scene to you in exquisite detail, but I chose not to since this is supposed to be a faith-based exposition.

I promptly put my hand up, hoping to halt her forward (and I mean *forward*) advance. I was also worried that her increased excitement might cause the strained buttons on the front of her dress to pop off and hit me in the eye.

"So, why are you in my room at this hour of the night?" I rhetorically inquired.

She stopped her awkward approach and answered, "I have something very urgent to speak with you about."

"Okay," I reluctantly agreed, as I sat down on the edge of the mattress, "so tell me about this urgent matter."

"Thank you," she breathlessly replied. "May I sit down?"

"Yes, of course."

But then Eleanor moved closer to me, indicating that she fully expected to sit next to me on the bed. "I'd prefer if you'd pull up a chair, rather than sit on the bed."

"Oh!" she feigned surprise. "Well, of course, darlin'. Whatever you desire."

Eleanor rolled out a chair from a desk, or perhaps the one where she was seated earlier in the shadows. She still managed to sit too close to me, as if she didn't want anyone else to hear our sensitive conversation in the otherwise empty room.

"I need to know if my husband, William, spoke with you," she said in a hushed tone.

Of course, you do, I thought.

"Well, Mrs. Crisp," I answered, making sure I addressed Eleanor by her married name, "I'm not at liberty to discuss confidential conversations I may have had with fellow Christians."

She sneered, "Are you some kinda priest or something, who can't talk about confessions people make?"

"No, I'm not a priest," I patiently explained. "It's just a principal of mine not to discuss private conversations I've had. For instance, I'm sure you wouldn't want me to tell anyone that you visited me in my motel room for this late-night chat."

She paused for a second and agreed, "I guess not..."

She paused another second and added, "Pastor Ripley probably shouldn't know I was here."

"Or your husband," I suggested.

"Oh, I ain't worried about that cuckold!" she said without a second thought.

"But you're worried that William may have spoken to me."

"I'm just worried that he may have misled you about an incident concernin' our daughter," she explained.

"Please tell me about this incident," I requested, trying to maintain eye contact.

"Well, a while back, I noticed that our daughter was becomin' more and more rebellious and misbehavin'. William, of course, insisted that it was normal behavior for a preteen to be acting out that-a-way. But when I heard her once use the Lord's name in vain, I asked Reverend Ripley to sit her down and have a talk with her. I was a-feared she was possessed by a demon!"

"A demon, eh?" I asked, raising an eyebrow. "So did the pastor agree to meet with your daughter?"

"Well, of course he did, silly," she shot back, "because nobody knows more about demons than the Righteous Reverend Harry C. Ripley!"

Ignoring her 'silly' comment, since I preferred it over 'sugar,' I asked the obvious, "So, tell me what happened."

"Well, I'm not exactly sure what went on," she admitted, "but I can tell you that my daughter has been right as rain ever since she met with the good reverend!"

Knowing the answer, I still had to ask, "Did you discuss the matter with your husband before you asked the pastor step in?"

Eleanor burst out laughing, apparently no longer concerned with anyone overhearing, "Of course not!" she exclaimed. "Weren't none of his business if'n you ask me! Besides, I knew William wouldn't agree."

"But the girl is his daughter too," I pointed out the obvious.

"Far as he knows, I guess," she said between her awful guffaws.

"Okay, let's not go there," I cautioned.

"Fine by me," she agreed with a grin.

"I'm going to meet with Pastor Ripley tomorrow to discuss his church," I concluded. "But I don't plan on asking him directly about your daughter."

"Good! I prefer you don't," she responded. "As far as I'm concerned, the matter concernin' my daughter is over and done with... Of course, you heard how pretty she sung today."

"Yes," I said with a sigh. "I don't think I've ever heard a more beautiful song about strychnine and snake venom."

"She rit that song herself," she proudly added with a smile, "since the original version had the N-word in it."

"Yeah, I'm familiar with the old minstrel version of the tune."

Getting back to her unfounded concerns, she surmised, "Well, I just want to be sure you don't interfere with the reverend or his church, based on any *unfounded* accusations."

"Mrs. Crisp, I represent the Assemblies of Christ organization and I can assure you that we do not have any regulatory power to interfere with a church's policies," I expounded. "AoC reps can only make recommendations based on our personal observations."

"That's good, 'cause you need not pay no attention to nothing my good-fer-nothing husband may of told you," she expressed in a flurry of double-negatives.

I purposely smirked and said, "Right, so are we done here?"

Eleanor boldly stood up in response and kicked away the rolling chair behind her, using one of her high-heeled shoes. The chair noisily crashed into the wall. She strutted another couple steps, until she was directly in front of me, then put her hands on her broad baby-bearing hips and confessed, "I sure wish my husband was more like you, Mister Blakely."

"Yeah?" I countered, standing up to face her. "How so?"

Eleanor motioned like she was going to place her hands on me, but suddenly withdrew, placing them back on her hips. "I like strong, tough-looking men like you," she hissed. "In fact, I bet a rugged man like you knows how to put a woman in her place."

"Let me stop you right there, Mrs. Crisp," I cautioned.

She ignored me and added, "I know a man like you wouldn't let his woman make important family decisions without his consent."

When I noticed her hands leaving her hips again, I warned, "It's definitely time for you to leave, Mrs. Crisp."

Eleanor's wandering hands reached up to the top button of her dress and quickly unfastened the hook, revealing a flushed neckline and upper chest. "Oh, Mister Blakely!" she begged. "Please put me in my place! Take control of me and teach me to respect men again!"

Eleanor leaned in close enough for me to taste her bated breath, so I nudged her away with the palm of my hand against her shoulder. She reacted with a pouty lip and offered, "But I won't tell anyone, Rossie, I promise. My lips are sealed, at least they will be soon enough, if you know what I mean."

I stood my ground and aggressively reiterated, "You should leave, right now, if you know what I mean!"

She purred, "Oh, so commanding and forceful! I love it!"

"I'm not joking, Mrs. Crisp."

"Nor I," she concluded. "If you can change my attitude towards men, the relationship with my husband would surely improve. He'd appreciate it almost as much as me."

I defiantly shook my head at her absurd proposition.

She then dropped to her knees in front of me and grasped my bare thighs, hugging me with her turned head planted against my boxers. "Please let me stay... Just for a while... Then I'll leave. I promise!"

I immediately reached down and grabbed her underneath her arms. I forcefully lifted her back to her feet and led her directly to the door. I then let go of her with one hand, but only to open the door and gently push her through the threshold.

"Good night, Mrs. Crisp," I told her once she was outside the room.

Before I closed the door, I heard her say, "Good night to you too, Mister Blakely. My number is on the nightstand. Text me if you get lonely!"

I then inadvertently raised her expectations when I reopened the door, but just long enough to place the DO NOT DISTURB placard on the knob... I'm sure she also heard me secure the chain and deadbolt inside the door.

Now alone in the room, I decided to take another shower – this time with cold water.

CHAPTER 5

It's quite annoying when you fall asleep, but soon get awakened by some odd sound. In my half-conscious state, I thought the sound I had heard was the alarm on the cheap digital clock atop the nightstand. But as soon as I lifted my head from the pillow, the sound went away.

And nothing is more annoying than when you fall asleep again and are awakened by same odd sound. This time I reached around the back of the nightstand and unplugged the clock from the outlet.

Satisfied that the red LED numbers of the clock were now extinguished, I confidently rested my head back onto the bunched-up collection of mini pillows. But before I closed my eyes, the buzzing sound erupted again.

I leaned over toward the nightstand and turned on the lamp. Everything seemed in place: the lamp, the clock, the telephone, and the heart-covered note from Eleanor. I concluded that none of these items were making the noise.

Consequently, I reached down and opened the drawer of the nightstand. But all I could see was the proverbial Gideon Bible. I smiled at its welcoming presence and decided to read a few passages.

As my fingers encircled the spine, the strange noise increased, and I instantly saw the head of a snake strike violently at my hand. I instinctively withdrew my hand and somehow managed to escape feeling the serpent's fangs pierce my skin.

I then used my other hand to grab a pillow and slam the drawer shut. I could hear the angry rattler frantically banging against the sides of the drawer as I quickly sat up on the edge of the bed, desperately trying to catch my breath. I stared lividly at the nightstand as it savagely shook, banging thunderously against the wall and bedframe, like it was going to burst apart at any moment.

I knocked all the crap from the top of the nightstand and then picked up the piece of fluctuating furniture. I moved it to the door and realized I had to set it back on the floor, because I had foolishly engaged the dead bolt and chain.

But once the door was open, I carried the nightstand out to the edge of the motel parking lot. I grabbed the handle and flung the entire drawer into the darkness. I could hear Gideon fluttering through the air and landing in some bushes. I assumed the snake was not far behind.

In the morning, I dropped by the front office. The same nondescript Desk Clerk was there, at least I think it was. A youngish maid, wearing a typical white uniform, was lounging casually in a lobby chair, twirling her blonde locks between her dainty fingers.

I marched up to the desk and inquired, "I don't suppose you know who put a snake in my room."

"A snake?!" the astonished clerk responded.

"Yeah," I confirmed, "someone put a live rattlesnake inside the drawer of the nightstand."

"Well, I don't know who would-ah done such a thing. I hope you didn't get bit or nuthin'."

"I almost did get bit!" I exclaimed.

"Sorry about that," apologized the clerk, "but I can't offer you no discounts on the room."

I rolled my eyes at the clerk's dead pan response. "I'm not asking for a discount. I want to know who put the snake in there."

"Nobody's rented that partic'lar room for weeks. Heck, the bed hadn't even been made up, as you know."

"Well, I don't think the snake has been in that drawer for weeks, unless it's been eating Gideon's Bible."

The Desk Clerk then looked over to the maid. "Hey, Stephanie, you know of anyone who had a snake in Room Twelve?"

Maid Stephanie smiled and answered, "Nope, the only snake I ever handled in that room was a trouser snake!"

Stephanie and the Desk Clerk broke out in hysterical laughter as I got red in the face.

"Very funny you two!" I interrupted. "I'm so glad you think my brush with death is so comical!"

The clerk stopped laughing and calmly informed me, "Oh, I don't think you would-ah died from it. Look up there..."

The Desk Clerk pointed to a shelf behind the counter. "We got a complimentary snake bite kit right next to the edible lube."

"That's very reassuring..." I mumbled.

"So, will you be staying with us another night?"

CHAPTER 6

I found my way to the basement of the Metz Pentecostal Church, and walked past a large classroom and a few unlabeled doors. I knocked on a door marked OFFICE.

I immediately heard "Come in! Come in!" from the other side.

Did I mention that Ripley was an older man, but still youthful in energy and extroverted in personality? Of course, you can picture him any way you'd like.

"Come in, Brother Blakely and take a seat!" he invited upon seeing me enter the small office.

Seeing him hunched over his cluttered desk (but not as cluttered as my desk, of course), I sat in an ancient chair opposite him and responded, "I hope I'm not interrupting anything."

Ripley pointed at a desk toy with five hanging ball bearings, which could be swung into one another. "No, I was just playing with this toy. Have you ever seen one of these?"

"Yeah," I observed, "maybe back in the eighties."

The pastor glanced up at me and responded, "Really? The eighties, huh? I think it's called Newton's Cradle."

"I guess because of physics or gravity or something," I concluded, with no real interest.

He swung a pair of the metal balls, causing a clacking sound. "You're probably right. All I know is, it fascinates me... If you let loose two balls on this side, then two balls will bounce off the other side."

"I see," I said.

"It actually helps me concentrate and remain focused," he explained, as he let a single ball smack into the others, causing one ball at the other end to swing out and clack back into the group.

I resisted rolling my eyes, worried that it could remind him of the toy.

He then leaned back in his chair and asked, "Would you like some coffee, Mister Blakely?"

I answered, "No thanks, I had a cup at the diner this morning."

"I have a Keurig and some of that specialty coffee from Ollie's Bargain Outlet," he added.

"That's okay," I assured him with a smile.

"My congregation purchased that coffee maker for me as a Christmas gift," he expounded. "You see, I live and work here in the basement of the church and the members see to my basic needs, which are few."

"As were the basic needs of Jesus and His followers, according to scripture," I pointed out.

"Indeed," he agreed, before ending the small talk. "So, what brings you down from Maryland to our little community?"

"Well, I was always meaning to come down and visit some small churches in West Virginia, but one of your members specifically invited me to your place of worship," I reported.

"And that member would be William Crisp," he surmised.

"Well, I'd rather not say," I said.

"I'm not asking you to say, or confirm anything, Mister Blakely," he confirmed. "William Crisp has been having some marital issues and I've offered to help the couple, but William is a very private man... A true man of faith, but private none-the-less."

"I understand," I replied. "We can only help our brothers and sisters as much as they allow themselves to be helped."

"And how exactly does the Assemblies of Christ help Pentecostal churches, if you don't mind me asking?"

"Well, we reach out to churches and their members, discuss any concerns that may exist, and offer recommendations or possible solutions to problems."

He leaned forward in his chair and informed me, "I haven't always been pastor here in Metz, but I don't recall ever asking to be associated with the AoC. I've always considered our church as Independent from... outside influences."

"I agree wholeheartedly, Pastor Ripley," I confirmed, maintaining eye contact. "The AoC is not a regulatory organization and has zero authority over your church. We only help churches that ask us for our assistance. In fact, if you wanted me to leave Metz this instant, I would honor your wishes."

He let that sink in for a moment before responding with a smile, "Don't be ridiculous, sir. I welcome your interest in our church and I believe in your sincerity and willingness to help in any way you can... Besides, I've got nothing to hide."

"No one has suggested that you do."

Ripley then pointed to a picture of a disheveled-looking man, which hung on the wall overlooking the desk. "Do you know the man in that photograph?" he asked.

"I was going to ask you about that," I answered with a quick glance at the frame. "I believe that's a picture of Alabama Pentecostal minister Glenn Summerford."

Surprised at my reply, he perked up and confirmed, "It is indeed, Mister Blakely! Glenn Summerford's picture is on my wall to serve as an inspiration to me."

"Of course, you know he's serving a life sentence for the attempted murder of his wife," I continued. "I heard she experienced a number of deadly snake bites."

Ripley shook his head and said, "Wrongly accused, my friend. It has been firmly established, as far as I'm concerned, that his wife had been possessed by demons. I believe she tried to kill herself with those snakes after word got out about her incestuous relations with her sons."

"I don't mean to argue, Pastor, but a jury found Summerford guilty based on evidence presented at a trial."

"I guess we'll just have to agree to disagree then, Mister Blakely, since neither of us attended the trial," he countered.

"Agreed, Pastor... But I am interested in your views on snake-handling and the casting out of demons."

Without missing a beat, he responded, "Being a man of faith, I'm sure you're not unfamiliar with the Book of Mark, Chapter Sixteen, Verses Fifteen through Nineteen."

"Of course, I'm familiar, and I respect those who view the gospel literally, but I think some verses are still open to interpretation, especially considering all the translations over the centuries."

Adding emphasis, by standing up from his chair, he quoted, "When Jesus rose from the tomb, He told his disciples, 'Go into all the world and preach the gospel to all creation. Whoever believes and is baptized will be saved, but whoever does not believe will be condemned. And these signs will accompany those who believe: In My name they will drive out demons; they will speak in new tongues; they will pick up snakes with their hands; and when they drink deadly poison, it will not hurt them at all; they will place their hands on sick people, and they will get well'."

Unphased, I reiterated, "Like I said, I am familiar with the Book of Mark."

"Well, what part of Jesus's words do you think are open to interpretation?" he challenged.

"Please Pastor, I'm not here to argue," I argued. "I only wanted to have a theological conversation with you."

Still standing, Ripley leaned forward and placed his palms on the desktop. "I'm not originally from

Metz, Mister Blakely. I was drawn here by the Holy Spirit when I learned that Metz had the highest percentage of drug overdoses and suicides in the state of West Virginia. When I first arrived here, I could sense that demons had taken control of the town and I became determined to stay here to drive them out."

"Where are you from, Pastor?" I asked.

"I'd rather not say. My work is here now, and my past is behind me."

"I can respect that," I added with a nod, "speaking from my experience prior to finding Christ."

Ripley walked around to my side of the desk and explained, "Since I've been a minister here, I've invited all residents to attend services at the church. If anyone who is possessed enters this sacred sanctuary, it won't be long before their demons are exposed and promptly exorcised."

I stood up to face him and inquired, "Does that include children?"

"What about children?" he countered.

"Would you attempt to cast out a demon from a child?" I repeated.

Ripley put his arm around my shoulder and stated, "Let me put it this way, Mister Blakely, I don't cast out any demons, unless it's in front of a full congregation of the church... where it can be witnessed by everyone in attendance."

CHAPTER 7

The Williams sisters lived in a sundrenched, peeling, white-washed Victorian house. You know, the kind that become funeral homes once the last descendants tire of maintaining them. But the Williams sisters were also high maintenance, according to Ripley, who gave me their address, which might explain why they remained spinsters into their golden years.

I carefully walked across the creaking slats of the front porch, knocking softly on the door once I successfully reached the threshold. The door soon opened, revealing the welcoming face of Dee Williams.

"Hello, Miss Williams, I presume? My name is Ross Blakely," I greeted, thankful that the salutation would work with either Williams sister.

"What can I do for you, Mister Blakely?" she asked sweetly, like she was going to bake me some cookies.

"Pastor Ripley gave me your address and said that you and your sister might be willing to talk about the church."

She danced away from the door frame and exclaimed, "Certainly! We love to tell people about our church and our wonderful pastor! Please come in!"

The interior of the old house appeared very dark, almost foreboding, as if it had originally been decorated by Lizzie Borden. Dee Williams led me to a candle-lit parlor room that reeked of Dollar Store incense and lemon-scented Pledge.

Winnie Williams was seated at a round wooden table, which was swathed in a royal blue silk covering. A small wooden box rested near the center of the table. Winnie watched patiently as we entered the room.

"Sister Winnie, this is Mister Ross Blakely," Dee announced. "He'd like to talk to us about our church."

Winnie stood and motioned politely with her hand toward an empty chair at the table. "I've been expecting you, Mister Blakely. Please come in and have a seat."

I sat down in the aforementioned chair, while the Williams sisters sat close together in chairs on the opposite side.

"Thank you, Miss Williams. I guess the pastor called you about my visit."

Winnie smiled and dismissively said, "Not necessarily."

"Oh... okay... Well, I hope I'm not intruding."

Dee spoke up, "Of course not!"

Dee looked at her sister, perhaps even kicking her underneath the table, which prompted Winnie to respond, "Yes, we're both very interested to learn how you intend to destroy our beautiful church."

"What?" I implored. "I mean, are you sure Pastor Ripley didn't call you?"

"Mister Blakely, we haven't spoken at all to the pastor about you," one or the other stated, I don't remember which.

"Well, I don't know where you got the impression that I mean harm to your church," I charged.

Winnie explained, "Considering the good that our church continues to do for this community, and the Godliness that Pastor Ripley represents, it only goes to reason that the Devil would want to destroy it."

I protested, "Well, regardless of my appearance, I'm not the Devil, I can assure you of that."

Winnie glanced down at the wood box, then back up to me, and concluded, "That's not what Rider and Waite have told us."

"Who are Rider and Waite?" I innocently asked.

Dee giggled and answered, "Tarot cards, silly."

"Wait a second," I cautioned. "Are you trying to tell me that Tarot cards revealed that I came here to destroy your church?"

Winnie confirmed, "The cards don't lie, Mister Blakely."

"Does Pastor Ripley know you dabble in the occult? I bet he doesn't," I gambled.

"We don't consider it the occult, because we only seek to channel God's word and not evil spirits," Dee expounded.

Winnie added, "According to James, Chapter One, Verse Five, 'If any of you lack wisdom, let him ask of God, that giveth to all men liberally, and upbraideth not; and it shall be given him'."

Her sister then threw in her Biblical justification.

"Yes, and Psalm 32 says, 'I will instruct you and teach you in the way you should go; I will counsel you with my loving eye on you. Do not be like the horse or the mule, which have no understanding but must be controlled by bit and bridle or they will not come to you'," Dee quoted.

"Literal readings aside, I think your pastor would interpret those verses differently and would probably advise you to only address God through prayer," I instructed.

"Would you like me to prove it to you, Mister Blakely?" dared Winnie. "I have the deck right here on the table."

"You may do as you please in your own home, Miss Williams, but you'll never prove to me that the God of the Apostles speaks to you through man-made Tarot cards."

"Believe what you like, Mister Blakely. But before we begin, please do me the courtesy of turning off your phone so that no negative vibrations interrupt our reading," Winnie requested.

I politely complied, pulling out my cellphone, turning it off and placing it in front of me on the silky table. Once Winnie was satisfied with my obedient gesture, she reached into the wooden box and withdrew a silk-covered deck of cards.

She placed the silk bundle on the table in front of her and moved the box toward Dee. Winnie carefully unwrapped the silk covering from the deck and placed the strand of silk back into the wooden box.

Winnie then proceeded to shuffle the cards in various ways, while Dee removed a pencil and a sticky-note pad from the box. Dee scribbled "Wisdom of the Tarot" on the top note.

Winnie showed me the deck and asked, "Would you care to shuffle the deck, Mister Blakely?"

I crossed my arms and answered, "No, thank you."

Dee pushed the notepad and pencil toward me and offered, "Would you like to write down a question?"

"Nope."

"Thy will, not mine, be done," Winnie proclaimed as she separated the cards into three stacks and named them: "The Father... The Son... The Holy Ghost."

Winnie then lowered her head in prayer. "Dear Heavenly Father, I entreat Thee to graciously bestow upon me Thy Heavenly blessing. Purify my thoughts and actions so that they may be guided and directed by Thy divine wisdom. Bless me with true knowledge and the ability to receive Thy everlasting love into my soul, so that I may sincerely seek out the truth in Thy Holy Name. Thank you, Father, Amen."

Working from the stack on her left, Winnie turned over the top card and placed it in front of its stack. She observed, "The Three of Cups represents to me abundance, joy, fulfillment and that something good is on the way... But to you, the reverse Three of Cups represents an overindulgence that creates problems. It also means that you allow idle conversations to adversely affect your perspective."

I hesitantly responded, "Ohhh-kay."

Winnie then turned over the card on the middle stack to display DEATH and placed it on the table in front of its stack. Dee let out a gasp and Winnie immediately lowered her head again in prayer.

"Dear Heavenly Father, I am part of Thy eternal plan and know that change is hard for me to understand. When change is thrust upon me, fill me with understanding and acceptance. Open my eyes so that I may see and understand the reasons for change and be ready to accept them. When change comes into my life, be with me, Father, so that I may find the comfort of Thy holy presence and accept Thy divine will. Amen."

Winnie looked up to me and prognosticated, "To man, the Death card represents fear that can only be overcome once you allow your ego to die on this earthly plane. You are in a state of limbo and depression...When the Death card lies next to the Three of Cups, it means you must change your lifestyle and start over again with new goals."

"In other words, you want me to leave town," I surmised with a smirk.

"The cards advise you not to resist sudden change and they recommend that you leave the past behind you," she continued.

"Like I said, you'd prefer me to leave town."

Of course, Winnie ignored me and proceeded to turn over the top card on the stack to her right. "The Seven of Wands represents to me that I am blessed with a strong character, and that my inner strength and courage allows me to handle any adversity. But to you, the reverse Seven of Wands indicates that your impatience leads to unwise decisions. When next to the Death card, the Seven of Wands means that you are going about things the wrong way and you should reevaluate your plans, Mister Blakely."

I appropriately rolled my eyes and responded, "Of course it does... Ladies, are we done here?"

Dee answered, "If you don't believe the Tarot, we have another method to communicate with God. Please give me a moment to fetch it."

When Dee rose and left the room, Winnie carefully put away the Tarot cards, wrapping the deck in silk and placing it back in the wooden box, along with the notepad and pencil.

Dee shortly returned to the parlor, proudly carrying (of all things!) a Ouija board. She delicately placed it on the table next to where she and Winnie were seated.

"A Ouija Board now? You can't be serious!"

Dee positioned the plastic stylus on the cardboard platform and reminded me, "God moves in mysterious ways, Mister Blakely."

"I think a children's game would be an exception to that creed," I countered.

Dee and Winnie each placed a hand on the stylus and bowed their heads. Dee prayed, "Dear Heavenly Father, please tell us if our guest has evil intent toward our church and its pastor."

I watched impatiently as the two women kept their eyes as shut as their minds, both still clenching the immobile stylus. After a couple minutes of the charade, I opined, "I guess God is still thinking about it."

"Hush!" Dee angrily blurted out.

And then the obvious occurred: The handheld stylus suddenly darted across the Ouija board and landed on the corner of the platform containing the word YES.

I shook my head and congratulated, "Good job, ladies. But which of you moved the stylus?"

"It wasn't me," confessed Winnie.

"Nor I," confessed Dee. "It was surely the Holy Spirit."

"Okay," I decided. "I think it's time I showed myself out."

I moved toward standing, but Dee cautioned me, raising her palm. "Hold on! I believe there is a direct message waiting for you! Please be patient."

I placed my hand on my phone and concluded, "If it's important, maybe God can just send me a text."

As soon as I was fully standing, the stylus started moving again, this time across the alphabet that was printed in the center of the board. I watched as the hand-held stylus skimmed across the platform to the letter P, then H, then O, then N, and finally rested on E.

Dee looked down at my hand, as it still rested on my cellphone, and suggested, "Perhaps you should check your phone, Mister Blakely."

I belligerently picked up my cellphone from the surface of the table, but my innocent action was met with horrific gasps and a shriek from the two women. Tucked underneath my cellphone, on the table, was the Tarot card depicting the DEVIL!

"The Devil card!" screeched Winnie.

"He really is a demon!" screamed Dee.

In utter disbelief, I stared down at the grimacing face of the horned Devil on the card. I noticed it was raising its right hoof, as if it were waving to me. Mocking me.

"I don't have time for parlor tricks!" I yelled.

Then I felt a brief breeze cross my face, simultaneously extinguishing all the candles in the room, and leaving us in darkness.

With my handy cellphone still in hand, I simply clicked on its light and headed straight out of the room. The women, of course, were still carrying on.

As I exited the parlor and started walking toward the front door, I heard the sisters begin chanting as they followed me. They continued chanting as I walked down the hall, opened the door, creaked across the porch, stepped down the steps, and headed for my car. Their words still haunt me:

> In the name of Jesus,
> In the name of Jesus,
> We have the victory!
> In the name of Jesus,
> In the name of Jesus,
> Satan, you got to flee!
> Who can stand before us,
> Who can stand before us,
> When we call out that name?
> Jesus, Jesus, Jesus!
> Jesus, Jesus, Jesus!
> We have the victory!
> Victory, victory!
> We have the victory!
> Victory, victory!
> Satan, you got to flee!

CHAPTER 8

It was dusk when I pulled away from the Williams home and drove toward downtown Metz. As I believe I mentioned before, there's not much to do in Metz after sundown. All the lights were off in the shops along Main Street and the only lights I noticed were some odd red and blue ones in my rearview mirror.

"How can I help you today, Sheriff?" I asked after I pulled over to the side of the street and rolled down my window to speak with the officer.

Sheriff Jeffreys leaned down toward my open window and inquired, "You Ross Blakely?"

"Yes, officer, I am." I confirmed. "Would you like to see my license and registration?"

"No, sir," he answered. "I only pulled you over because I got a call from the Williams sisters."

"Were they singing?"

"No," he said without blinking an eye, "at least not the sister I spoke with on the phone concerning an assault she says took place at their home."

"An assault?!" I exclaimed.

"Spiritual in nature, I suspect," he cautioned. "But I thought I'd better talk with you anyway, so they know that I followed up on their complaint."

"Well, I assure you, Sheriff, the only reason I visited them was at the suggestion of Pastor Ripley."

"I believe you, Mister Blakely," he said. "The Williams sisters are known for being a bit... How can I say it? A bit eccentric at times."

I mumbled, "Eccentric is putting it lightly."

"Yeah, they're just not right in the head," he agreed, as he leaned in a bit closer to me. "Anyway, they did mention that you had a lot of jailhouse tattoos, so apparently they weren't wrong about that."

I shook my tattooed head in capitulation. "No, they certainly weren't wrong about that."

For good measure, the Sheriff added, "Well, you know what the Bible says about defiling yer body with such markings?"

"Yes, sir, I am very familiar with that passage, but Pastor Ripley didn't seem to have any concern about my tattoos when I met with him earlier today."

"Is that right?" he cross-examined.

"Yeah, but he probably didn't want to judge me based on something I did prior to being saved by my Lord and Savior Jesus Christ."

The Sheriff thought for a second, then straightened up. "I guess there's somethin' to be said about repentance."

"I guess."

He graciously concluded, "Well, sir, concerning the complaint, I'm gonna let you off with a warning, since the Williams sisters seem reluctant to press any charges."

"Well, bless their hearts," I responded. "How kind of them."

As he turned to walk back to his cruiser, the Sheriff added, "You take it easy now and don't cause no more trouble in town, ya hear?"

After a deep breath, I put my turn signal on and intended to pull back onto the street, but my cellphone buzzed, and I decided to stay put.

"Hello? Yeah, this is Ross... Hi, Bill... Yes, I can meet you at the diner. I'll be there in a few."

CHAPTER 9

Phyllis's Diner was packed that evening, but it wasn't hard finding Bill Crisp and his daughter tucked away in a booth near the back. I took a seat in their booth, opposite the two Crisps, and observed Bill nursing a glass of ice water, while Amber was sipping a milkshake.

"Hey, Bill, nice to see you again," I greeted. "Your wife couldn't make it?"

"Nah, she's busy with housework," he supposed.

Out of the corner of my eye, I noticed two young men exit the booth across the aisle from us. Bill would later inform me that these were the Sheriff's sons, Edward and George.

When Edward passed by the table, he turned his head to his brother and remarked, "Check it out, George. I guess our little town is where old gang-bangers go after they serve their sentences!"

LOL, right?

George added, "Yeah, Eddie, maybe dad should see if there's been any escapes up in Hazelton [Penitentiary]."

The brothers proceeded down the aisle, laughing like the demented fools they were.

Bill then informed me, "Don't pay them boys no mind, Ross. They're the sons of the Sheriff and they think they can do and say whatever they please."

"They don't bother me," I admitted. "In fact, I just had a conversation with the Sheriff, and I made it clear that Pastor Ripley has no problem with me being in town."

Bill took a moment to drink some of his ice water, then asked, "How's your investigation comin' along, if you don't mind my askin'?"

"Not bad," I answered, since I didn't mind him asking. "But I don't want to draw any conclusions until I attend a full service at the church. As you know, I got there late yesterday evening."

"You missed the best part when we praised God at the beginning."

"Yeah, I heard..." I confirmed.

Amber slurped the last of her milkshake through the straw, belched, and then suddenly blurted out, "I ain't sure it was the reverend that done beat me that day!"

Bill and I both looked at Amber, who was now shaking her paper cup to confirm its vacant state. Bill tried to ask, "Excuse me, baby girl..."

Amber continued, "I said, I'm not so sure Pastor Ripley was the one who whooped me."

Bill patiently pointed out, "But you said Pastor Ripley did meet with you that day."

"Yeah," she explained, "he pulled me outta Bible class and we talked in his office, but I don't know if'n he follered me back or not."

My turn: "Well, Amber, what do you remember after you left the pastor's office?"

"Alls I remember is..." she started, then asked me, "Hey, Mister, what'd you think of that song I sung at the end of the service?"

"Umm, it was beautiful, honey, especially the part about the snake venom."

"Thank you! I wrote them words, you know!"

"Yes, I'm aware of that," I told her. "But can we get back to what you remember about the day you were disciplined?"

"Disciplined?" she enunciated.

Bill instructed, "Mister Blakely is talkin' about you bein' beat, dear."

"Ha! You talk funny, Mister," she observed. "Anyways, all I remember is, someone grabbin' me from behind and draggin' me into a dark room. This person blindfolded me with somethin', put cloth in my mouth, and taped me up to a chair!"

"This mystery person didn't say anything to you?"

"Nope. Not a word, Mister," she remembered. "The person just started-ah whoopin' on me with a belt until I felt a demon leave my body!"

I paused to allow her to collect her thought, then asked the obvious, "You actually felt a demon leave your body?"

"Yes, sir, that's why I figgered it was the pastor who whipped me, 'cause he's good at riddin' people of their demons."

I tried not to act too surprised, then concluded, "Well, Amber, you're a brave girl and I'm glad you told me everything you can remember."

She proudly perked up and offered, "I'd show you my welts, but I think they all faded away."

"That wouldn't be necessary," I consoled her, "because I believe what you told me."

Bill drank the last of his water, crunched a chunk of ice between his teeth, and said, "Thank you for comin' by, Ross."

"No problem," I responded. "I wanted to grab something to eat anyway... If I can get the waitress's attention..."

In unison, Bill and Amber yelled, "Hey, Phyllis!"

CHAPTER 10

Oh, did I mention that I parked in my usual place adjacent to the diner? You know, the nearby lot where I need to walk through the dark alley? Yeah, that one.

Anyway, I was about halfway through the alley when I heard some rumbling behind a dumpster. I figured it was rats. I figured right.

Edward and George Jeffreys stepped from behind the dumpster to confront me.

Edward flicked a rotten banana peel off his shoulder and postured, "Well, if it isn't the old Chicana with the prison tattoos."

I held my empty hands up, palms toward the brothers, indicating that I did not want any trouble. "Listen guys, I don't want any trouble. I'm just passing through."

George explained the dilemma. "Yeah, well, that's the problem, isn't it? The Sheriff asked us to show you what happens to nosey outsiders who cause problems in our town."

Dramatic pause.

"Go ahead and show me, boys," I invited, raising my fisticuffs. "But I'm going to warn you, I got more than just tattoos in prison... Prison is also where I learned to fight."

The boys both rushed me, demonstrating that they wouldn't dare fight me one-on-one. George then demonstrated that he learned to fight by playing Street

Fighter Turbo on Super Nintendo. He tried throwing a wild hook at my head, which I easily ducked beneath; and I returned a solid punch to his midsection that instantly brought him to the ground in a state of groaning breathlessness.

Edward fancied himself as a kickboxer, probably from watching too many MMA bouts on YouTube. He began dancing around me, crouching with his fists just below his eyes, and almost tripping over his fallen brother. "Go ahead! Come at me, man! I'm ready!" he threatened.

"I thought you were the aggressor, boy!" I snarled as I kept an eye on his antics. "Remember, I'm not the one who wanted to fight."

Edward tried to send a couple of lame kicks in my direction, but they weren't even close. I mocked, "Didn't your daddy teach you to fight, boy?"

My comment caused him to get angry, as was intended, and Edward came in tighter and tried another kick. This time his slow-motion shoe came near enough to me that I was able to grab it with both my hands - and flip Edward into the air like a dandelion spur. His face hit the side of the dumpster, but he quickly jumped back up, as did his lame brother.

As soon as the boys were back on their feet, they reached into their pants pockets and produced matching pocketknives. They approached me again, after ensuring that the blades were drawn and not the knives' handy corkscrew or screwdriver attachments.

"If you boys knew how many shanks I wrenched from the hands of real killers, you wouldn't be trying this," I warned.

George began waving his knife back and forth in front of himself as he drew closer to me. "That's not a switchblade, you fool," I laughed. "What if you slash me with the wrong side?"

I then gave Edward a demonstration of a real kick, as I swirled around and caught George's knife hand with my boot. The loosely held knife flew harmlessly into the air upon impact. George was dumbfounded at the sudden loss of his weapon and I was easily able to deliver a left, right and an uppercut to his confused skull.

As George dropped unconscious to the ground, I moved my attention to Edward, whose confidence had fallen exponentially. He tried the poke-a-dope method with his knife, repeatedly jabbing the blade toward me as if he hoped I would give up and run myself into it.

I soon realized his half-hearted thrusts were defensive in nature, so I quickly reached over and grabbed his wrist, twisting his arm behind him until the knife fell to the ground. I held his empty hand behind his back and lifted his arm up until his shoulder dislocated. He yelped in pain.

I then spun him around and landed a hard punch squarely on his nose, which caused his eyeballs to cross and roll upward, until his eyelids covered them, and he collapsed onto the cement beside his snoring brother.

"Tell your daddy I said hello."

When I reached my vehicle, I noticed a note underneath a windshield wiper. I pulled it off and got into the car.

After starting the engine, I turned on the dome light and looked at the note. It contained a crudely drawn map and the words: COME SEE ME ABOUT RIPLEY.

CHAPTER 11

Through hill and holler (i.e., hollow) I drove my car through the twisting West Virginia countryside, trying my best to follow the directions of a drawing that looked more like a fractured spider web than a map. Plus, it was night.

I later learned that the Sheriff was looking for me at the motel that evening, but all my belongings were safely stashed in my trunk and I had no intention of returning to that snake pit.

Eventually, I pulled up to what I believed was my destination, which turned out to be a dilapidated farmhouse in the wilderness. I exited the car and walked toward the front door. No one left the light on for me.

The door suddenly burst open and revealed an older man sporting a shotgun. I jumped backward and began waving the paper note like it was a white flag of surrender. The man then lowered the shotgun and greeted me accordingly, "I was hopin' you'd drop in. My name is Cecil Polhill!"

I shook his free hand and introduced myself, "And I'm Ross Blakely. It's nice to make your acquaintance, Cecil."

"Well, come on inside," he invited. "It's the quickest way to the back porch. I gotta fire burnin' out yonder."

After he placed the gun against the threshold, I followed him through the ground floor of the decaying house. We exited the back door and walked out onto a porch, which was illuminated by a decent-sized bonfire. There were a couple of cheap lawn chairs near the fire and we made use of them.

I glanced around at what I could see of my surroundings and immediately focused on what looked like a large moonshine still, complete with rusting barrels and copper tubing. Also, there appeared to be a crate of glass bottles next to the still.

I pointed at the heavy metal contraption and asked, "Is that thing for real?"

He laughed and answered, "Yes, siree, it's the real McCoy!"

"That's an interesting choice of words."

"That there still is how I git by these days," he explained. "Times is hard, Ross, and a man has to earn money anyways he can."

He paused for a moment and then offered, "Hey, you wanna share a bottle of shine with me?"

Slightly surprised, I politely declined, "No thanks, I quit drinking last year."

"Suit yerself," he responded despondently. "You don't know what you're missin' out on."

I changed the subject by mentioning, "According to the note you left on my car, you wanted to speak with me about Harry Ripley."

"Yep," he confirmed, "I was at the diner downtown and I heard you was lookin' into the preacher and his shenanigans."

"Okay, so how do you know Pastor Ripley?" I asked. "Are you a member of the church?"

"Oh, hell no!" he exclaimed. "But I guess you could say I'm part of his so-called outreach program."

"Outreach program?"

"Yeah," he confirmed. "Ripley is always goin' around the streets of Metz beggin' folks to attend his church. But if you decline his invite, then he'll come a-knocking on yer door as part of his outreach program."

"Interesting…"

"That's why I always have my trusty twelve-gauge settin' right by the front door."

"I assume his outreach visit to your place didn't go so well," I assumed.

"You're derned right, it didn't go too good!" he bellowed. "Ripley tole me he'd heard about my still and how I sell my shine throughout this here county."

"So, he asked you to stop, right?"

"Hell, no! He didn't *ask* nuthin'!" Cecil corrected me. "Ripley *said* he was gonna send the Sheriff up here to tear apart my only means of makin' a livin'!"

"Did the Sheriff ever drop by?" I followed up.

"Ah-'course not!" he answered. "That Sheriff and his kin are nuthin' but a bunch of cowards! Sheriff Jeffreys wouldn't dare set foot on my property, let alone touch my still!"

I shook my head and told Cecil, "Yeah, well, I've had the pleasure of meeting some of his kin and I don't disagree with you."

"I ain't one to judge," he informed me, "but his daughter's the worse. She treats that motel like it's her own private singles club. Then she's always the first one in line fer church the next day."

"Yes, I've met Stephanie too," I added, realizing he was talking about the self-professed handler of 'trouser snakes.'

"Did you know she's the official snake wrangler for the church?"

"Excuse me?"

"Yep, she cares for the rattlers that the church uses in its services."

"Oh my," I mumbled.

"You didn't know they handle snakes at that church?"

I tried to clear my head of the unkind thoughts that raced through it, then admitted, "I guess I suspected it, but I haven't personally witnessed it."

"Well, you keep goin' to that church and eventually you'll see the snakes brought out and git passed around like the head of Medusa," he expounded. "In fact, there's a lot of snakes in that church and they all ain't the reptile variety!"

I thought about the Sheriff and his spawn, and then pondered the missing member of the clan. "How about the Sheriff's wife? Have you got anything good to say about her?" I asked with a small glimmer of hope for the Jeffreys.

"The Sheriff's wife, you say? Ha! She done left Stephen Jeffreys when she caught him spending a little too much time with that Crisp woman."

"Wow!" I exclaimed as my mouth dropped open in shock. "You don't say?"

"I do say!"

Once again, my mind became cluttered with the peripheralities per Polhill. I forced myself to get back on track. "But getting back to the pastor, did he stop bothering you?"

"For the most part, but I hear he's still harassin' other townsfolk," he explained. "Like he keeps goin' out to that No-Tell Motel, hoopin' and hollerin' at folks he thinks is sinnin' inside their romper rooms."

"Actually, I did hear something about that," I recalled.

"Also, there's a lady that owns a clothin' shop in town and Ripley goes through her stock every week, looking fer anything that's not modest enough fer his particular tastes."

"Well, I haven't heard that."

"Yes, sir, just another example of Ripley interferin' with people's livelihoods," he stated. "But you ain't heard the best part of his visit to my place!"

"And that is?" I bit.

Cecil grinned and answered, "Well, Ripley said my shine was a health threat to the community, but I told him that my shine has only blinded a couple folks, as far as I know."

I laughed and said, "Really, you told Ripley that?"

"Yeah, but that ain't the funny part," he continued. "Before he left, I seen him sneak one of my purple bottles inside his coat!"

"Ha!" I laughed again. "Now that is funny!"

Both of us broke up in a fit of laughter and I felt we were starting to bond.

"So, are you gonna share a bottle with me or not?" he asked again.

"You know what, Cecil?" I acquiesced. "I think I will try some of your product. If it's good enough for Pastor Ripley, then it's good enough for me!"

"You got that right, my friend!"

But I had to ask, "It's not gonna blind me, is it?"

As Cecil stood up to fetch a bottle, he concluded, "Hey, if'n you're Pentecostal, no kind of poison's gonna harm ya, right?"

I lost track of time as we passed around his purple bottle of potent booze. My eyes soon captured the scene in an eerie soft focus, the fire crackling and sending its embers into the air while flashing its orange light upon Cecil's withered face.

Cecil then used the fire light to study my devilish face. He asked, "So, can you tell me how you got all those crazy tattoos?"

"Sure," I agreed, looking out into the flames. "I took the wrong path when I was a kid in Tucson... I started out life as part of a street gang and ended up working for some evil mobsters. But my life changed when my niece fell in with some drug dealers and God Almighty helped me to rescue her... You know, I don't mean nothing by it, but you sort of resemble one of the dealers..."

He spoke right up: "Well, I can assure you, I ain't never left the state of Wild and Wonderful West Virginia!"

I turned to him with a friendly smile and confirmed, "I know you're not the guy, Cecil. Anyway, I think that man's younger partner eventually took him out."

Cecil then fell quiet again, drifting into a state of silent reflection, as though he was comparing my life to his. I watched as his rather jovial mood became one of somber despair.

Cecil looked down at the empty bottle in his hand and sullenly reflected, "You know, some people joke that shine is like their rheumatiz medicine, but it really does help me with mine. I got terrible pain in my feet and my hands. I can hardly function sometimes, let alone sleep at night."

I leaned closer toward him and cautioned, "You know, Cecil, maybe it's not arthritis you're suffering from. It could very well be diabetes, which is nothing to mess around with."

He shook his head and added, "All I know is, sometimes my fingers are so numb that I start droppin' stuff, or my feet get to trippin' over each other."

Obviously concerned, I asked, "When's the last time you were seen by a doctor, Cecil?"

Cecil looked at me and admitted, "I can't afford no doctor. Can't say as I trust 'em anyway."

"You have Medicare, right?" I inquired.

"No, I don't have no Medicare!" he declared. "I've never taken a dime from the government and I ain't startin' now! Cecil Polhill don't need no government assistance!"

I explained, "Whether you need it or not, you're an American Citizen and you're entitled to health care. If you don't use your benefits, the government will just squander the money on something else."

Cecil started to cry, "I'm scared, Ross. All I got here are my cats. I don't have no family anymore."

Tears welled up in my eyes too. "Calm down, Cecil, I'm here right now. I will help you in any way I can, my friend."

Cecil looked up to the sky, tears flowing down his wrinkled cheeks. "You know, Ross, I farmed this land with my daddy when I was a boy and I continued farmin' it long after he passed. I farmed it and farmed it and farmed it, until my old body broke down and I just couldn't do it no more... I just feel so damned worthless..."

I stood up and moved my chair next to Cecil. I rested my hand on his trembling arm. "You're not worthless," I told him. "You're not worthless to me and you're not worthless to God... Cecil, would you let me pray for you?"

He looked at my face and confessed, "I've never been a religious man, Ross, but I figger it can't hurt."

"Hey, I trusted your moonshine, so you can trust me with this," I said.

"Okay, Ross..."

We both lowered our heads and I prayed, "Dear God, please lay your healing hand upon my righteous friend Cecil. He has led a hard life, Lord, working the fields of his ancestors, and now finds himself alone as he reaches old age... Like the crops that flourished in the fields for most of Cecil's life, allow him to grow like the Cedar of Lebanon, planted in the house of the Lord and glorifying the courts of our God. May Cecil still bear fruit in old age and remain fresh and green... The Lord is upright; He is my rock, and there is no wickedness in Him. Amen."

Cecil echoed, "Amen."

We both sat in silence, holding each other's hand.

After a few minutes, I announced, "Well, it's getting late and I probably should be going... But you'll be hearing from me soon enough. I won't forget you, buddy."

Cecil shook his head and uttered, "Umm, forgive me for not mentioning this earlier, Ross, but you probably shouldn't drive after drinking so much shine."

I rolled my bloodshot eyes and then remembered the effort it took for me to carry my chair over next to Cecil. "You're probably right," I agreed.

"I got me a guest bedroom, if you'd like to spend the night," he offered. "Besides, I wouldn't mind havin' company, if you know what I mean."

"You know, Cecil," I testified, "I've also lived by myself for most of my adult life, but I stopped feeling alone the moment I invited Jesus Christ into my life."

He nodded and acknowledged, "I shall take that under advisement, my friend. Like you said, I need to trust you on matters of the soul."

After I grabbed my suitcase from the car, Cecil showed me upstairs to a small nondescript bedroom, which was likely his boyhood room. I placed my suitcase on the Superman bedcover and said, "Thanks, Cecil. This will be fine. I appreciate your hospitality."

"You're quite welcome," he responded. "If'n you need anything, just let me know. The bathroom is down the hall."

"Okay. Goodnight, Cecil."

Cecil began to walk out of the room, but suddenly stopped in the threshold. He turned around to face me and he struggled to say, "I been thinking about what you told me, being lonely and all... Can you tell me how you got Jesus in your life?"

I excitedly told him, "Well, of course I can! Come sit next to me on the bed!"

We sat together and commenced with Cecil's Salvation.

CHAPTER 12

Although the evening had ended on a high note, I still experienced a very restless night and my mind treated me to a nightmarish odyssey:

I'm on a city sidewalk, at least I think I am, because I hear people walking past me and talking. I also hear traffic buzzing past me on one side. I'm frightened.

I'm frightened because I'm blind and I'm lost. I'm stumbling along with my arms outstretched, trying to feel for obstacles in my path. I cry out, "Help! Can someone help me?! I've gone blind and I can't find my way!"

Someone bumps into me and I hear laughing.

I beg, "What?! Why are you laughing?! Please help me! I think I drank too much!"

I feel someone grab ahold of my collar and begin shaking me. I hear a youthful male voice, and am showered with spittle, as he yells in my face, "Who are you, anyway? Some drunken clown? You need to leave this town!"

"What town am I in?!" I plead, "Is this still Metz?"

The masculine voice erupts into more laughter, exclaiming, "Wino, are you kiddin' me?! Metz is a ghost town! Ain't nobody lived there in years!"

"Ghost town?" I mumble in confusion.

"Yeah, Metz is a ghost town!" he squalls. "Are you some kinda ghost? You lookin' for a house to haunt?"

I desperately shake my head, hoping he will release his grip on my collar. I don't dare try to fight him, because I can't see... "No, no, no, I just need some help! Please, I've gone blind!"

Then I hear a woman approach in heels, and I feel the man's hands release my clothing, as if he has been pushed away. The woman's voice demands, "Hey, boy, you leave this man alone! He ain't botherin' you! Get yerself down the street! Git now!"

"Fine!" the man responds as his footsteps begin to stomp away. "You take care of the drunken bum!"

The gentle touch of a woman's fingers soon surrounds my arm, and she says, "Come this way, sir. I own the fashion store here. Let me see if I can get you some help."

The sounds of the city street fade when we walk inside the building... Then I hear a familiar voice.

It is Ripley.

"Miss Price, I've only found a couple dresses that are immodest."

"Then I shall remove them from the rack, Pastor," the woman responds.

Not understanding what I'm hearing, I speak, "Is that you, Harry Ripley?"

Ripley answers, "Is that you, Ross Blakely?"

"Yes, yes, pastor, it is I!"

I hear him step toward me and say, "Well, I didn't recognize you with that blindfold on."

"Blindfold?" I ask.

"Here, Ross, let me remove it."

I feel his hand brush my face and then quickly pull something from my head. Bright light instantly strikes my eyes and I fall to my knees. But I don't fall in front of Pastor Ripley.

When my eyes adjust to the light, I realize I am outside, alone, and in a wooded area... Directly in front of me, planted in the ground, are three empty crosses, like the ones on Calvary. I begin to pray.

CHAPTER 13

"Wakey, wakey, eggs and bakey!"

What? I stirred myself partially awake and looked toward the door. The blurry image of Cecil Polhill eventually came into focus as I tried to sit up in the bed.

"Where am I?" I managed to murmur.

Cecil grinned and answered, "Remember you slept here last night?"

"Cecil?" I asked, still trying to shake the cobwebs from my dazed mind.

"That's me!" he confirmed. "I fried up some eggs, if you're interested... Ain't really got no bacon though."

"How about coffee?"

"Yes, sir! A whole pot full!"

"Thank you, I'll be down in a minute."

After breakfast, I said goodbye to Cecil and reminded him that he hadn't heard the last of me. If I accomplished anything on this mission, it would be to make sure Cecil sees a doctor and gets the help he needs.

The winding roads proved easier to navigate in the daylight, as I headed back toward town. However, I still didn't have the confidence to drive these dirt roads while talking on the phone.

So, when my cellphone rang and I noticed the name SAM on the screen, I pulled off the road to take the call. Sam, of course, was my older sister, calling me from Tucson.

I smiled when I answered the call. "Hey, sis! What's going on in Tucson? How's my lovely niece?"

My lovely niece, of course, was Jennifer, who I saved from the drug dealers that basically were keeping her hostage in a nasty trailer park just outside the city limits.

Samantha responded, "Hello, brother. Jenny is fine and sends her love, as always."

"So, what's up?" I asked.

Samantha confessed, "I had a strange dream about you last night, Ross. I dreamed you were in some kind of trouble. I saw you wandering through the wilderness, searching for something."

"Really?" I said with surprise. "There's nothing to worry about, Sam. I happen to be in the mountains of West Virginia, but I'm not wandering around the wilderness."

Samantha concluded, "Oh, well thank God you're safe! Jenny and I are praying for you, I hope you know that."

"I most certainly know that," I confirmed. "And I'm always praying for you guys too... Okay, sis, goodbye. I love you."

When I placed the cellphone onto the passenger seat, something caught my eye outside the car. I did a double-take and gasped at what I saw on the hill outside the passenger window.

On a brush-covered hillside was a set of three crosses.

The lower crosses on the sides were painted blue and the tall center cross was painted gold.

[Note: These crosses are known as Coffindaffer Crosses and they can be seen throughout Appalachia and some other parts of the country, as erected in the 1980's by West Virginia Reverend Bernard Coffindaffer.]

Before I knew it, I was out of my car and climbing the wooded hillside, in order to reach the crosses that I had seen in my dream.

Out of breath and covered in mud and briars, I immediately collapsed onto my knees in front of the gold center cross. I raised my arms to the heavens and prayed aloud:

"Dear Lord, help me while I seek the truth today. Please give me the wisdom to break through the obstacles and lies that Satan has placed in my path. Do not let any unwholesome gossip enter my ears, but only what is helpful for me to build others up according to their needs.

"Grant me, Lord, the insight to know what I ought to know, to love what I ought to love, and to praise what I ought to praise. Do not allow me to judge according to the sight of my eyes, or to pass judgment according to what I hear from dishonest men.

"Help me discern, with true judgment, between things visible and spiritual. Help me, God, to see people the way you see them, and to be filled with compassion, even when someone is doing wrong against me. Help me to respond with love, instead of anger or bitterness. God, you make the impossible possible. Thank you for filling me with your love and freeing me from the compulsion to wrongly judge others. Father, help me to be mindful that it is not my place to judge others. I am no better than they are. You will bring down and lift up as you see fit. I love you, Jesus. Amen."

CHAPTER 14

It was dusk when I drove into the empty parking lot of the Metz Pentecostal Church. The church sanctuary was also empty, save for the pastor at the pulpit rehearsing his evening sermon.

As I walked down the center aisle, Ripley noticed me, looked up from the podium, smiled, and greeted, "Mister Blakely, you're here early!"

I smiled back as I approached, and said, "Well, I didn't want to miss anything this time."

Ripley motioned toward the front pew with his hand and invited, "Please take a seat. There's something I'd like to discuss with you."

As I sat down, I watched him carefully circumvent the empty aquarium with the purple bottle perched on top, in order to reach the front pew. He sat down next to me.

He placed his hand on my leg and looked me in the eyes. "First off," he began, "I want you to know how terribly sorry I am about the poor reception you've received in our town, especially from the members of this congregation."

"But I can understand how folks can be suspicious when a stranger comes to town," I admitted.

"That's still no excuse for their bad behavior," he explained. "If you remember, when we met, I told you that I welcomed your interest in our church and I continue to believe in your sincerity and willingness to help in any way you can."

"I appreciate that," I answered.

He nodded in agreement, but sternly added, "What I'd like to do tonight is, march some of these judgmental church members straight over to you and have them apologize."

I shook my head in disagreement. "Oh, no. Please don't do that. I wouldn't want to embarrass anybody. If anyone's going to apologize, it'd be better if they did so on their own."

Ripley thought for a moment and concluded, "Well, I don't see that happening. In fact, I have a troubling foreboding about tonight's service."

"Why do you say that?" I asked.

"You might think this is silly," he explained, "but I was praying at my desk today when I accidentally knocked off the toy with the metal balls. The toy smashed onto the floor and the balls rolled across the room out of my reach."

"A simple accident, Pastor," I suggested.

He looked toward the stage and added, "The metal balls shouldn't have rolled anywhere, Mister Blakely. Remember, they had strings attached."

"So, you believe that was some sort of omen?"

He looked back at me and confessed, "I think those metal balls represent members of this church, Mister Blakely, and their faith ought to keep them together."

"With no strings attached?"

"Yes, with no strings attached."

CHAPTER 15

The congregation was soon filing in and filling in the sanctuary. From my seat in the front pew, I noticed Edward and George Jeffreys approach the pulpit where Pastor Ripley was standing. I heard Edward address Ripley: "Pastor, Sister Stephanie wants to know if you want her to bring in the serpents. She's got them out in the truck."

Ripley curiously studied the boys' faces and answered, "Not tonight, boys. I don't feel as though the Holy Spirit has called us to observe that sign today. There are more pressing matters at hand."

The boys turned around and immediately saw me sitting in the front pew. There was a moment of uncomfortable silence as the three of us observed one another. For instance, I observed the bruised faces of the sullen boys.

George then extended his hand toward me and I rose to shake it. "Please accept our apologies for the fight last night," he apologized. "We clearly misjudged you and hope you forgive us."

I smiled and replied, "Of course, all is forgiven! But I wasn't aware that I hurt you guys so badly."

Edward then took his turn shaking my hand and explained, "Not all of these bruises are from our fight, Mister Blakely."

"Oh..."

George added, "In fact, do you mind if we sit up front with you this evening?"

I motioned with my hand toward the empty front pew and invited, "Guys, I'd be honored."

As we took our seats, I glanced back toward the other pews and noticed Sheriff Jeffreys and Stephanie Jeffreys seated near the center of the sanctuary, both displaying scowls on their church-goin' pious faces.

Speaking of church-goin' pious faces, it wasn't long before the Williams sisters and Brother Andrew took their regular places on the stage behind Ripley. From somewhere behind me, I could hear Amber Crisp acting up and her mother shushing her. But no one, other than the brothers, bothered to approach me, greet me, or otherwise acknowledge my presence. Oh, well...

Pastor Ripley cleared his throat and projected:

"There are six occasions in the Gospels that describe instances where Jesus cast demons out of people. In all six instances, Jesus did not seek out the demonized people. Jesus simply went out and preached the Gospel - and the demonized came to Him!

"Both Matthew and Luke wrote about demon possession. They wrote that a man may claim to have rid himself of a demon, while boasting that Christ and the Gospel are with him. And though his once-possessed body may then seem to be empty, it is not empty of sin!

"It is said that these abandoned demons will then walk through dry, deserted places, seeking rest and satisfaction, but will find none. They will then join other evil spirits, looking to disturb and cause mischief among men, until they finally, as a group, return to the original host.

"Yes, when these demons return to exert their full fury once more, they enter into this so-called holy man again. They are more violent and cruel than before; worse than the Devil, himself! In this state, the man will drop all pretenses of religion and holiness. They will return like dogs to the vomit and like swine to wallow in the mire!"

As if on cue by the mention of dogs and swine, music burst out from the trio at the back of the stage, specifically an original hymn called "Sevenfold." The Williams sisters' voices were instantly joined by the rest of the congregation (except me, of course, who didn't know the words):

The Spirit of the Lord shall rest upon me
The Spirit of wisdom and understanding
The Spirit of counsel
The Spirit of might
The Spirit of knowledge,
And of the fear of the LORD!
These are the spirits,
The spirits of God,
These are the spirits,
Held dear by our Lord!
The Power of Jesus,
The Power of Jesus,
The Power of Jesus,
The Power of Jesus,
The Power of Jesus,

The Power of Jesus,
The Power of Jesus,
Sevenfold!

The final refrain became a soft chant that was repeated over and over, as Pastor Ripley began to shout above this "The Power of Jesus" refrain. He spoketh:

"There's a shameless and adulterous woman amongst us who has torn apart families, dishonored her faithful husband, viciously beat her own child, and continues to deceive and blame others for her evil lecherous deeds! Rise by the Power of Jesus!"

Eleanor Crisp looked up in shock from the mirror in her compact, dropping her lipstick on the floor, as everyone in the church turned to stare at her. Bill and Amber looked away in shame.

Amber then instinctively tried to grab ahold of her mother's leg, but only managed to grab a shoe, as Eleanor's body was lifted into the air, literally with no strings attached. The congregation gasped, along with me, as I tried to make sense of the shrieking woman who was now dangling helplessly above us all.

Ripley continued shouting, his face as red as the communal blood of Jesus:

"There's a cruel father and a debauched daughter in our fold, who are filled with such hate and meanness that they will go out of their way to harm any Christian or kind person who threatens their tyrannical control over this God-fearin' county! Rise by the Power of Jesus!"

The flailing bodies of Sheriff Stephen Jeffreys and Stephanie Jeffreys shot into the air above the pews and hung in suspension near Eleanor Crisp. I wanted to cover my eyes from the incredible horror unfolding before me, but my rattled brain would not allow it. I had to witness, and gasp, and react, just like the other terrified parishioners. The screams of the entrapped trio near the ceiling echoed throughout the sanctuary and throughout my muddled mind.

But Ripley didn't stop there. He turned around and pointed directly at the Williams sisters, proclaiming:

"And finally, there are two charlatan siblings inside our place of worship who practice Satan's very own witchcraft, but still dare to judge others with their outrageous holier-than-thou piousness! I say, rise by the Power of Jesus!"

Dee and Winnie abruptly stopped chanting and looked at each other in fear, just before their bodies were thrust into the air. Five flailing figures now dangled demonically, traumatized with terror, while the congregation cowered.

I'm sure my face was just as flushed with fright as what I observed when I looked over at the panic-stricken palettes of the two brothers.

"Come on boys, let's get out of here!" I yelled.

The three of us jumped up and planned to escape the chaos by exiting along the side aisle of the pews, but Ripley noticed our attempted departure and shouted, "Hold on there, Blakely! The best is yet to come!"

We turned around in unison to watch as Ripley raised his arms to the heavens and commanded:

"Listen to me, you unclean spirits, who will not let our people talk or hear for themselves! In the name of

Jesus Christ, I command you to come out of them and never enter them again!"

--- The bodies of the five began to spin like weightless toy tops, their heads flinging back and their mouths gaping open, as dark swirling smoke streamed upward from their quivering lips to envelope the church in a wretched fog that stunk like sulfur, just before the five fell hard to the floor and started flopping and shaking uncontrollably, frightening the other church members who fled from the places where the twitching bodies had landed, but still watched as the five anguished faces began choking thunderously while their mouths stretched open to an inhuman wideness, coughing up nasty looking frogs which jumped aimlessly across the slatted floor, accompanied only by the back doors of the church suddenly bursting open allowing the entry of a monstrous wild hog and a devilish red-eyed black dog, which began violently consuming the fleeing frogs, while the panicked people tried running for the doors to avoid the swine, the hound, the stench and the convulsing bodies before them. ---

The dark smoke soon made it impossible to see anything.

CHAPTER 16

Once Pastor Ripley took his place just outside the doors of the church, the congregation began leaving. Ripley made small talk as the people exited, mostly accepting thanks and appreciation for the sermon, while responding "Bless you", "You're welcome," "See you next time," etc.

I watched as the three members of the Crisp family exited the church. Bill enthusiastically shook Ripley's hand.

"Thank you so much, Pastor," Bill said. "Forgive me for ever having doubted you."

Ripley smiled and responded, "I forgive you, Bill."

Eleanor added, "Pastor, would it be too much to ask if you'd renew our marriage vows?"

Ripley nodded and agreed, "I'd be happy to, Eleanor."

Amber also had to get a word in, asking, "And can I sing at the next service?"

"Of course, you can, Amber!" Ripley complied. "I look forward to it, honey!"

The Jeffreys clan was the next to emerge from the church.

As the four approached, Ripley told them, "I'd like to see you folks start sitting together again at services."

The Sheriff answered for the group, "Oh, we plan to. Don't we, kids?"

Edward, George and Stephanie all happily nodded their heads in agreement. The family then walked past the pastor and into the parking lot.

The Williams sisters and guitarist Brother Andrew then came out of the church.

Ripley informed them, "Hey, I just received a special request for the next service."

Brother Andrew answered, "Anything you want, preacher man. You know that."

Ripley explained, "Amber Crisp is wanting to sing again, and I'd like you three to help her put together something special."

Dee excitedly responded, "We'd love to, Pastor Ripley!"

Winnie echoed, "Yes, I look forward to it! Amber has such a sweet voice!"

"That's great!" Ripley exclaimed. "You folks be careful goin' home, you hear?"

"Yes, sir," acknowledged Brother Andrew.

Once everyone had said their good-byes, Pastor Ripley re-entered the sanctuary. I was the only person remaining in the church, having made my way back to the front, near the pulpit.

As Ripley approached me, I picked up the purple bottle from the top of the aquarium and looked at the label, which read POISON.

I grinned at Ripley and said, "I think I need a drink after that service… I assume this is the brew of Cecil Polhill?"

"Your assumption is correct," he confirmed with a laugh. "After all, you can't judge a bottle by its label."

"I think that goes for the both of us," I agreed.

"Indeed, Mister Blakely."

I pulled the cork from the bottle and took a swig.

I passed it to Ripley, who also took a drink, and then handed the bottle back to me.

Ripley said, "In the words of Pentecostal prophet Stanley Frodsham, 'If you will indeed judge yourself, you shall not be judged'."

I replaced the corked bottle to its resting place and added, "Amen, brother. Amen."

After a moment of reflection, Ripley asked me, "So, does the Assemblies of Christ have any recommendations for our little church?"

I looked at his confident face and quoted Ecclesiastes: "Eat your food with gladness, and drink your shine with a joyful heart, for God has already approved what you do."

We briefly embraced.

I then said, "Goodbye," as I turned to walk away.

"Go in peace, Ross."

ABOUT THE AUTHOR

After an unillustrious print journalism career in southwestern Pennsylvania, Rich Bottles Jr. moved to West Virginia at the age of 32 to pursue a career in technical writing. During his spare time, he wrote secular novels and short stories for ten years, before finally finding his calling with faith-based novellas and screenplays. In addition to developing his Christian novellas "Godsend" and "Pent Up!" into screenplays, he also wrote the screenplay for the first Ross Blakely mystery entitled, "Strange Friends."

A Ross Blakely Mystery

STRANGE
FRIENDS

GARY LEE VINCENT

PROVE YOUR LOVE

GARY LEE VINCENT